A Predisposition for Madness

xx for Madness xx

Aurelio Rico Lopez III

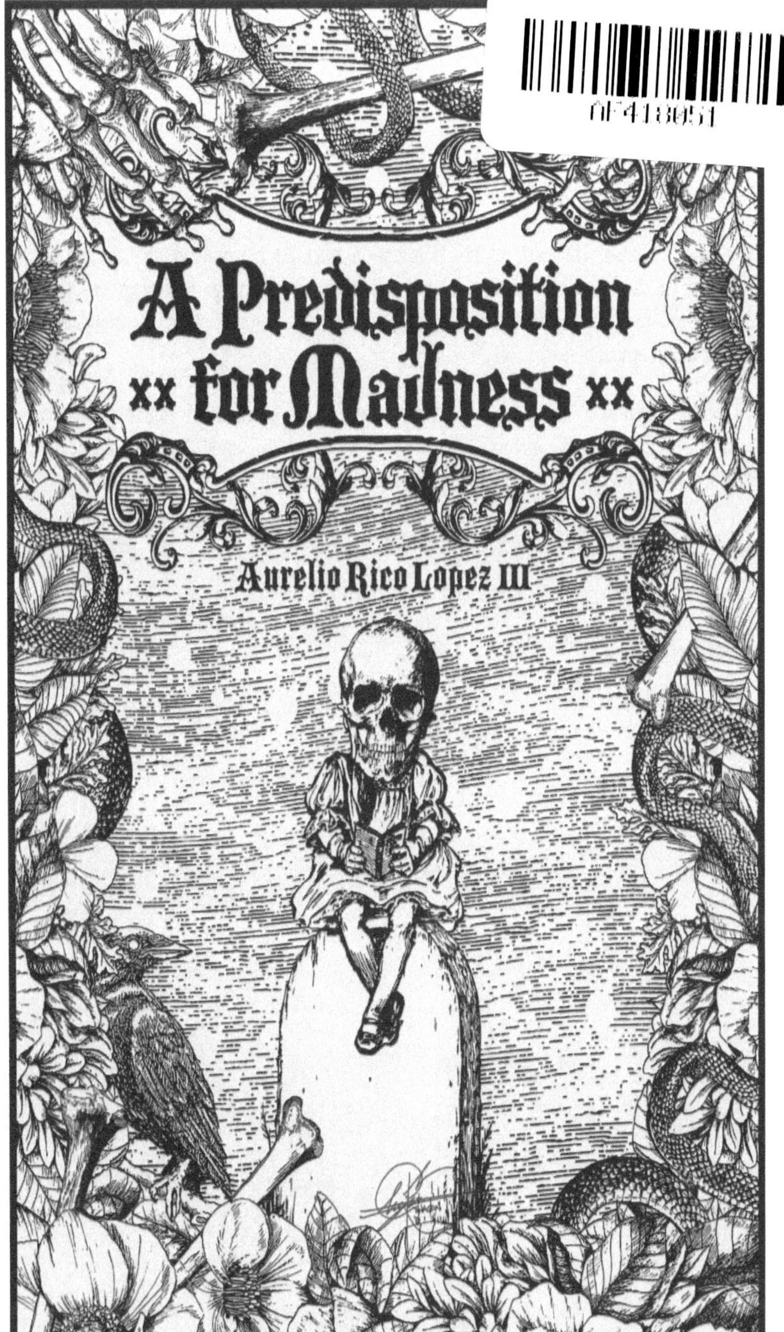

ISBN: 9798721991509

Massachusetts – Philippines
0013

A Predisposition for Madness

by Aurelio Rico Lopez III

This collection
is dedicated to all the brave frontliners
of the COVID 19 pandemic.

Contents

A Predisposition for Madness

All the Signs

The way he eyed her,
his loud voice and corny jokes...
He might as well have been
a silverback
pounding his chest
to gain her attention.

He introduced himself;
his real name?
Probably not.
Not that it mattered; it never did.
More jokes, no doubt rehearsed.
Lame pick up lines.
Still, she laughed politely.

"Your place or mine?" he asked,
no finesse, just unwavering
alcohol-induced confidence.
She smiled and uttered
a rehearsed line or two
of her own.

Hours later, as she lay beside
his lifeless, bloodied body
in his apartment,
she gazed into his glassy,
empty eyes.

Disappointed, disheartened,
and confused.

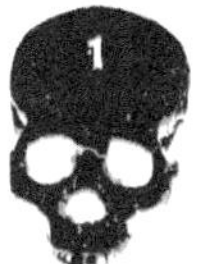

What went wrong?
She could have sworn
he was the one.

Primitive

Horde approaches,
weapons raised
to fire at moment's notice.
Aircrafts patrol airspace
while large metallic vessels
circle the seas like
schools of gigantic
predatory creatures
of lore and legend.

Amidst mushroom cloud
of dust and debris,
lone figure emerges from crater.
An army descends
upon its location,
prepared to unleash
utter devastation.

Being surveys the multitude
with disdain.
Such primitive inhabitants
bent on destruction
and ruin.
Eons squandering resources
and laying waste
upon each other.

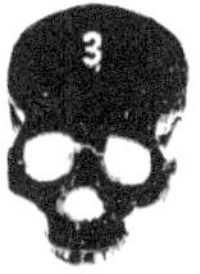

Reluctantly, figure raises a hand
and readies to defend itself.

Perhaps the annihilation
of these creatures
was unavoidable after all.

Restless

Voice hardly registers,
as if a thick glass pane
stands between them.

Separation.

Attempts to focus on
the document
on the table,
but tears melt words into
obscurity.

The pen,
inches away.
Unable to reach out.
Fear, guilt –
one or the other –
pins his useless
appendage down.

Like a delayed flight,
voice
finally reaches its destination.
Figure in white coat
speaks gently.
"It's been months;
she isn't going to wake up."

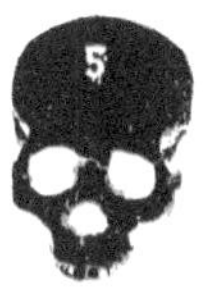

Chompers

Luke's left eye had
almost swollen shut.
He had been successful
in avoiding Scott and
his lackeys all week,
but the big kid had been
waiting for him at the
schoolyard today.

The time Luke spent
with Chompers almost
made him forget
the beating he'd suffered
at the hands of
the school bully.

Luke unzipped his bag and
unwrapped his latest treat –
a dead possum he'd found
by the road
on the way home.
Probably run over by
Mr. Harrison
who drove like a madman,
especially when he
was flat-out drunk.

Chompers waded at the
bottom of the muddy ditch
and made short work
of the offering.
Luke had been bringing
them for the past four months –
lizards, worms,
the class hamster that died
last spring.
But as Chompers grew,
so did his appetite.

It was getting dark.
Luke touched his left shoulder
and winced.
Scott had kicked him there,
hit him when Luke was
down and begging him
to stop.

Chompers looked up,
expecting another
offering, but there was
none left to give.
And then, Luke's lips
curled into a smile.
He zipped his bag
and limped home.

Luke was sure he could find
Scott's number in the
phonebook at home.
He'd love to show that jerk
exactly what
his friend Chompers
could do.

The Warning

Moon hangs low
in the horizon,
burdened with secrets.
Heavy stalks part
as dark silhouette
moves past,
stirring wisps of fog.

A second figure
traverses the field –
unwary traveller
who regrets
not heeding
the drunken ramblings
of the men from the tavern.

Lantern light wavers,
blinking in the evening
like a glow worm
in the grass.
Heavy breathing and
clumsy footfalls
add to the cacophony
of night insects and
restless frogs.

Deep within the field,
drawing close,
inhuman screeches
and glimmers

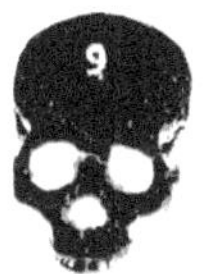

of feral eyes.
Within moments,
the lantern's flame
vanishes as night
claims one more secret.

Family Tree

I drag the old man
through the dark woods,
discarding him
beneath the shade
of a large mahogany tree.
He is a logger
who has, without a doubt,
violated this forest
countless times.

The man whimpers
and backs away,
cowering against the trunk.
Icy winds stirs the branches
overhead;
a cloud shields the trees
from the pale silver light
of the moon.
Patiently, I inform
the old logger how he
and his kind have
driven me and
my family from our homes,
how ceaseless deforestation
has forced my ilk
to the brink of extinction.

My family cannot
look blindly upon atrocities
inflicted on us.

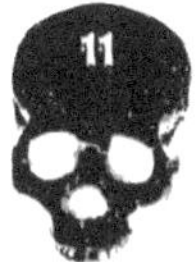

No longer!
We will not stand idly
as our homes are
stripped away
one by one.
Branches above us creak;
the logger gasps and looks up.
Moonlight illuminates the
forest floor once more.

What's left of my kin
glares at him from
every limb and branch.
The snivelling wretch
pleads for mercy,
but sharp claws
rake the tree's rough bark;
dozens of inhuman eyes glower,
demanding justice...
starting with this one.

Haunted

The air is ripe with
stench of piss and refuse.
Sickly mold grows
in the cracks between
discolored bricks.
Flies buzz, jostling around
a discarded jar containing
God knows what.
Disease-carrying cockroaches
scuttle about aimlessly
in the open,
having never before
encountered a shoe
or a rolled-up magazine.

Newspapers spread
on the ground like
the legs of crack whore.
A pauper's bed, blanket,
dining table, and outhouse
decorated in newsprint.
Headlines, breaking news,
Hollywood gossip –
meaningless.

A filthy, calloused hand
clutches an empty bottle
of cheap elixir,
unable to let go of
blissful intoxication.

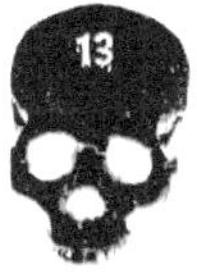

Phantoms haunt
this desolate stretch,
hardly afforded
a passing glance.

The Madman

Tattered clothes
and greasy skin,
face hidden behind
long, unwashed hair,
he wanders city streets
a stray dog,
inhabiting damp alleys,
roadside curbs,
underground subways,
and public washrooms.

The madman rambles on,
muttering to himself,
pigeons, and passers-by.
Shoulders slumped,
carrying the heavy
weight of a dark secret.
In sunken eyes
reside knowledge.

He is a ghost,
invisibility his curse.
But time is short;
the end, near.
So the madman
continues to whisper
the secret to anyone who
cares to listen.

The Last Straw

It was fifteen minutes
since the detective left
and the last police car drove off.
The house felt empty,
hollow.

Ruby's eyes wandered
the stack of dishes,
unwashed in the kitchen sink.
She'd get to them tomorrow;
too exhausted.

Left cheek still burnt where
he'd slapped her
three hours earlier.
Makeup and sunglasses
would not hide the bruise.

It had started years ago,
heated arguments that led
to shoves, which later
became punches, kicks,
and beatings.

At first, she thought
it was his struggle with alcohol,
but her husband seemed
more than capable even
without help from the bottle.

She'd grown tired
of all the questions from
friends and neighbours
who must have known;
how could they not?

When she lost the baby
two weeks ago –
an accident, he insisted,
without a hint of remorse –
that had been the final straw.

Carefully devised plan
set into motion.
The police would search for
her missing husband
but would never find him.

Jaime was dead,
poisoned over dinner
like the rat he was.
Authorities had searched
her home, but found
nothing out of the ordinary.

The faucet dripped on the dishes.
Her marriage had been
heading down the drain anyway.

Luckily, the police
forgot to check
the garbage disposal unit.

They Come Out at Night

They come out at night
when the moon ascends
and the day's warmth
drains away like life
out of a dying man.

Behind shuttered windows
and barred doors,
families cower.
Mothers hold their children
close to their bosoms.

From deep within
underground burrows,
they emerge
by the hundreds,
restless and hungry.

Each night,
the buzzing chorus
of the ravenous swarm
drowns screams of agony
and gunshots.

Dawn breaks;
more people are missing.
There is no time to mourn,
only to prepare for
night's dreaded arrival.

They come out at night.
A small child whispers a prayer
as dusk approaches.
She seals the shutters,
hoping to see the light
of the next day.

Rounds

Eyes weary,
half-empty cup of coffee
in hand,
he barely notices the parade
of doctors and nurses
walk past,
morphing into a milky white
blur.

He blinks,
stares down at his paper cup,
drink cold and flat.
The scent of lemon
lingers in the hall,
barely masking
Death's presence
who visits the sick,
the infirmed, the confined,
more often than
any one physician.

Eyes weary,
half-empty cup of coffee
in hand,
Death sighs, stands,
and continues his rounds.

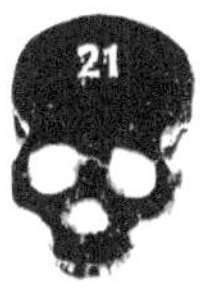

The One Time Danny Should Have Picked Truth

Dark, paneless windows
like hollow sockets of a skull
stare out into the street.
Weathered fence
leans inward,
its wooden slats
reminiscent of spikes intended
to keep the enemy out –
or in this case, in.

The yard is a refuge
for weeds and vermin.
Amidst a patch
of creeping wild vine,
lies an old yellow frisbee
abandoned by its owner,
who decided
its recovery was not
worth the risk.

Young boy stands in front
of foreboding house,
before the sagging porch.
His friends gather on
the opposite side of the street,
their voices
urging him onward.
The boy swallows;

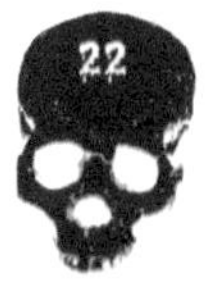

a drop of sweat traces
his cheek.

He takes one step forward.
Go inside and
get it over with.
Just grab the hairbrush
from her bedroom dresser.
Another step.
You can do this;
nothing to it.
The stories are just tales,
stretches of imagination,
nothing more.

Yet, small heart beats
furiously inside his chest.
Lead feet.
One final step.
Tall tales, nothing more.
Trembling hand reaches
for the doorknob and twists.
Don't worry,
he tells himself
as door creaks open.
The old lady always
sleeps in the afternoon.

Beyond These Walls

Soldier stumbles through the field
under the starless sky,
shadows loping close behind,
feral snarls filling the night.

Empty sheath,
slaps against the man's thigh;
sword lost in the forest,
among dead comrades.

Ambushed from out of nowhere,
enemy emerging
from the trees, the ground,
the very darkness itself.

Unnatural foe,
spoken of only in whispers
who seek bounty, not of coin
but of blood and bone.

In the distance, torchlight.
Wall draws closer.
Soldier's legs fail, exhausted,
and he crashes to the moist earth.

Claws immediately seize his feet
and drag him back.
Fingernails desperately rake
the frigid soil.

Prayers fall on inhuman ears,
fangs tear through flesh;
screams silenced even
before the first arrow is shot.

That Which Flows in Our Veins

We buried Mother today,
placed her in a pine box,
and lowered her into the earth.
Father said a few words
hollow, though they were,
void of conviction.
That's when I knew
she'd be back.

Our family –
shunned by one generation,
detested by another.
It is our blood;
some say it is tainted, cursed.
But we have long-accepted
which has been
bestowed upon us,
for it is what it is.

Call it what you might,
but there is magic in our veins;
but what people
cannot understand,
they fear.
And that is why
we buried Mother today.

She'd gone to the store
to purchase cereal and milk.
As she crossed the road,

a truck barrelled
out of nowhere.
People claim it was an accident,
though no measure of effort
was made to find the driver.

Father and I sit at the table
set for three.
He is silent as always.
A faint knock at the front door,
and I know she is home
just in time for dinner.
People fear what they
cannot understand,
but there is magic in our veins.
It is what it is.
I greet Mother with a kiss,
ignoring the dirt on her face.
She smiles.

Dire Consequences

The seer warned us;
she had seen the signs –
how the chickens laid eggs
in batches of three and how
none of Missy's pups
survived the first night.

We were told to offer
one of the goats
to the spirits of the land,
but Father scoffed.
If the spirits wanted a goat,
they should have raised
one themselves, he said.

Upon hearing
Father's answer,
the seer shook her head sadly,
almost mournfully,
saying there would
be dire consequences.
Father said no more and
paid her to be on her way.

A week had passed,
the warning fading away
from memory like an
early morning fog in the fields.
Almost all was forgotten
until Father accidentally

stuck his hand beneath
the plough.

He lost three fingers that day,
and though I was but a boy,
I couldn't help but
remember what the seer
said about the chicken eggs.
Batches of three.
Unable to work the field,
my father ordered me
to take on some
of the heavier duties.

Many night's I'd come home
palms ripe with blisters,
neck and arms raw
from laboring
under the unforgiving sun.
Whining, Missy would pad
next to me,
pink tongue lolling,
but I would push her away.

It was a month later when
I learned Mother was pregnant.
Father, it seemed,
had taken more intimate duties
whilst I worked the field.
Upon examination,
the doctor – the same one

who had amputated
Father's fingers –
said Mother was to expect
triplets.

The announcement
should have been met
with joy and celebration,
but I glanced down at Missy,
unable to hide my dread.
Batches of three.
The seer spoke of
dire consequences,
and I could not help but imagine
Missy's still, lifeless litter.

Heavy Rainfall and Strong Winds With a Chance of Murder

The radio had called it the storm
of the century.
Scott knew the media
exaggerated stories to
drum up ratings,
but for once, he agreed
with the forecast.
This was the big one;
he had never seen
weather like this before.

A flash of lightning
revealed the oak in the yard.
Scott's father had planted
the tree when he was
a young man.
Now the oak lay uprooted,
on its side like a fallen
prize fighter after
a hard left hook.

Gusts of icy wind
howled from the broken
upstairs window,
and he had to be careful
not to slip and cut himself
on the shards of glass
scattered across the floor.

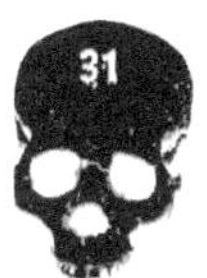

The downpour sounded
like the chorus of
an angry mob.
The house groaned;
boards popped and protested
against the continuous
onslaught of the storm.
Rain leaked from the roof;
a shutter ripped free
from one of the windows.

The sledgehammer made
dull, heavy thuds on the steps
as Scott made his way
downstairs.
It was, indeed,
the storm of the century.
It would surely make
finding her
that much harder.

Slippery Descent

For weeks,
cold fists pound
against bunker door.
How much longer
could the undead keep it up?
He closes his eyes
and imagines their
rotting bodies huddled,
flesh tearing bit by bit
as they slam thick,
unyielding steel.

The fluorescent bulbs
cast a glare
in the enclosed space.
Supplies, running water,
food to last months.
The first few days
pass without incident.
They were grateful
to have survived;
they had even celebrated.

Not a single one of them
could have anticipated
the festering psychosis,
slowly creeping,
taking root,
and finally corrupting
the minds of men.

In many ways,
this slippery descent
into madness was worse
than the infection itself.

It began with the voices –
people they once knew,
who could not possibly
have survived as they did.
At first, they paid no attention
to the seemingly
sourceless articulations,
but they were everywhere –
in the walls, in the drainage,
even in the toilet –
murmuring,
laughing, screaming.

Whispers,
orders to commit horrible,
unspeakable acts.
Inside the bunker,
the survivors ignored the voices,
but it was only a
matter of time before
they turned on one another.

Weeks pass.
Outside, the pounding
continued,

dozens of decaying fists
hammering against steel.
But they could not
drown the voices
inside the last
remaining man's head.

Jungle

Buildings rise proudly
above the city streets –
man-made canopies
over concrete jungle.
In place of animal calls,
automobile horns,
screeching tires,
and the rhythmic clang
of a train on its tracks.

Herds of pedestrians
gather around watering holes,
ordering drinks after
a long day's work.
Men strut and flex
in an attempt to impress
females who pretend
not to take notice.

Drunken teenagers hang out
on the bridge,
howler monkeys,
screaming obscenities
at anyone foolish enough
to cross their territory.
A police car rolls by
red and blue lights flashing,
and the troop
disperses hastily.

Meanwhile,
unnoticed in a dark
section of the city,
half-concealed in shadow
under the flickering lights
of a streetlamp,
a predator crouches,
beside helpless prey.
Knife catches the light,
shimmering.
Jungle built from
blood demands its share.
Such is the way of
the wild.

The Package

Escorting the caravan
through the mountain pass,
troop of armed men
flank the carriage,
wielding swords, maces,
crossbows, and axes.

The air is thin and cold,
yet no one complains,
for there are more
pressing concerns
than the comfort of
a mere few.

Priest clutches his crucifix
and mutters prayers
into the howling wind.
He raises a bottle and
splashes blessed water
on the carriage.

The four horses forge on,
their mighty breaths pluming
in great white clouds
before them,
blessedly naive of
the wickedness they tow.

A large white mist
coats the ground

like a fleece.
The pace is slow,
and the destination
remains distant.

The monastery sits
atop the mountain.
Only the priests who
dwell within its walls
know how to rid
the kingdom of this evil.

Wolves howl and snarl
in the distance.
The horses stomp their hooves,
and neigh anxiously,
refusing to travel any further.

Priest continues
reciting prayers.
The men glance nervously
up and down the path.
Dust and debris shower
down the mountain face.

A pale-faced soldier makes
the sign of the cross;
weapons drawn as
menacing shadows converge.

The enemy has arrived
to reclaim their master.

Expectation Versus Reality

So this is Hell,
I tell myself, immersed in
a sea of flames –
the place I was taught
as a young boy
to fear while our
local priest fondled
my genitals behind his
locked office door
on Saturday afternoons.

Hellfire is bright
like a hundred spotlights
trained on you.
Your eyes burn,
and blinking doesn't help
because your tears
have long since
dried up.

There are others –
occupants of Hell.
How could there not?
I can hear them,
though that might
just be my screams
ringing in my ears.

So this is Hell
where I am to suffer

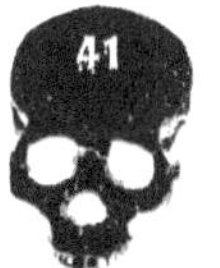

eternal damnation.
At least it isn't a world
behind a locked
oak door.
At least I do not see
the guilt on my
God-given parents' faces
when they chose
someone's word
over the testimony
of their own
flesh and blood.

So this is Hell.
I expected worse.

Pruritus Fatalis

Under the bright lights
in the apartment bathroom,
the stranger unbuttons
his shirt,
revealing a red lesion
just below his neck.

Nails rake dry skin
and the result is one
of temporary bliss,
but the itch returns
the instant the scratching
stops.

Fingers dig deeper,
harder
until angry, raw flesh
is exposed;
but God!
The itch is still there,
ever present.

Vaguely aware of
blood rolling down chest
like droplets
on a car windshield;
his mind is too
focused on ridding
himself of the gnawing
sensation.

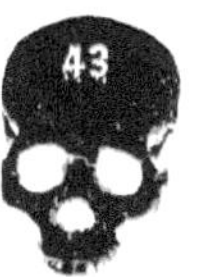

Furiously clawing,
he storms out
the bathroom,
into the kitchen where
he picks a steak knife.

Police arrive at
the apartment the next day.
An officer is first
on the scene and
later interviewed
by the lead detective.

Suicide –
What else?
But what goes unnoticed
is the red welt on
the officer's cheek,
one that was not there
this morning.

End of the Line

They say when Death
comes for you,
it takes the form of your
deepest fear.
There are no real experts
on the subject,
and all the authorities who
can confirm or refute
the concept are either
lying in a morgue
or rotting six feet under
in a casket.

There are those
who argue that Death
comes in the guise
of a friend or loved one,
a friendly face.
Again, a lot of this is
conjecture with no
real evidence.
I suppose if the Ferryman
were to disguise himself,
his appearance would
hardly matter;
when the Reaper comes,
you're pretty much
screwed anyway.

Yet, as I lay in

my hospital bed,
attached to snaking
intravenous lines,
machines that inflate and
deflate my tired lungs,
and tubes that ensure
I do not inconvenience
the medical staff by
shitting and pissing
all over myself,
I cannot help but wonder
about these things.

Help From the Stars

Faraway light pulsates
like a firefly against
backdrop of night.
Toward planet's surface,
a craft plummets,
careening across the sky,
navigation systems shot
and hull torn.

Mister Lamar's cattle,
unaware of impending
obliteration,
dream of leaping over
the moon or whatever
it is cows dream about
these days.

Meanwhile, Betsy Smith
sits alone on the porch,
asking the heavens for a sign.
She glimpses the drifting light,
Smiles, and decides
to go with Ethan to
next Friday's dance.

The New Normal

It begins a decade
after the big pandemic
our fathers used to
prattle about when
we were just kids –
ten years after our folks
observed social distancing
and needed to be told
to wash their hands,
when grocery stores
somehow ran out
of toilet paper.

The new sickness
makes the old-timers
long for SARS and Covid.
Now, in addition to
wearing masks and
hand washing,
people are being ordered
by the government
to lock their doors
and trust no one.

The National Guard,
dressed in hazmat suits,
patrol deserted streets,
enforcing curfews.
Businesses go bankrupt,
world economies crumble,

and industries grind
to a standstill.
Schools, parks,
places of worship close.
There is no miracle cure,
no vaccine.
Not this time.

Army vehicles transport
bodies by truckload
for incineration.
No words of comfort,
kind messages,
or teary-eyed mourners.
Not a single flower
is offered to the deceased.
There simply isn't the time.
A gunshot echoes as
the disease claims
its latest victim.

The Sarcophagus

Navigating blindly
inside unchartered
maze of tunnels;
each stretch and corner
identical to the last.
Might as well be
running in circles.
Nevertheless,
pulse racing and
adrenaline pumping,
he continues his flight,
splashing through
filthy puddles and
breathing in the foul air.
The batteries in
his flashlight
have long run out,
yet he dares not discard
the torch.
Finally, he slams against
an impenetrable barrier.
His fingers search
desperately for a latch,
a door, a secret entry
but finds none.
He turns, back to the wall
to face the darkness.

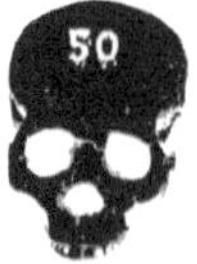

In the gloom,
the unmistakable stench
of death, heralded by
the scuttling sound
of a thousand insects.

Of Your Own Flesh

Hold your children close to your breast
flesh of your own flesh
that they may grow knowing
what it is to be loved
and shall love in return.

Hold your children in your arms
for they are our dreams
of brighter days,
bridges between today and tomorrow,
magical shimmers of hope.

Hold tightly to your children
and ask that they forgive
our wrongs and shortcomings.
Raise them not to stumble blindly
on the same misguided,
trodden paths as we have,

For a day may come
when our children will break free,
unable to bear our loving caress.
They will flee from our tender words
and abandon our most fervent
of prayers,
leaving us gazing upon our very
reflections.

The Murder

A crow
perches on barbwire fence,
cawing,
beady eyes gazing
at the immense field
beyond metallic roost.

Two, three, four crows
balance on barbwire fence –
winged performers
flapping,
scanning vast
golden sea of corn.

Five, six, seven crows
convene on barbwire fence,
birds black as night
under the glare
of one
bright afternoon sun,

A dozen crows
gather on barbwire fence,
by the scent of the dying drawn,
and Nature's promise
of morsels
after a feast.

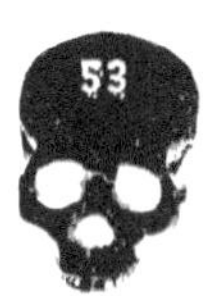

Manananggal

Darkness encloses
as I walk the wooded path
to my home.
The sun has long since set,
and the wind whistles through
gnarled branches above –
a sound both
familiar yet haunting.

Above the din of
evening's breath,
another noise
catches my attention –
the flapping of large wings.
I stop and cock my ear
to listen, but it is gone.
Believing myself to have
misheard the current of air
through these age-old trees,
I carry on.

I had taken but a few steps,
and there it was again –
closer.
It must be a large bird,
I told myself,
for sizeable fowl
are common in the area,
and one could have lost

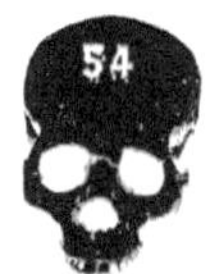

its way, flying blindly
in the gloom.

Yet, though the night
was not particularly cold,
I felt an icy chill
to the very marrow
of my soul,
for old wives still
speak of the manananggal
and other creatures
that color the tales
of drunkards, spinsters,
and old men whose minds
have lost their grip on
reality.

But twice more I heard it,
the beating of large wings,
and though my pace
had quickened,
each time the sound re-emerged,
it drew nearer.
My own heart fluttered
as though it had wings
of its own.

I tore through the night,
risking injury to myself.
I believed a broken leg

would be better
than the grisly alternative
for I, too, had heard the stories
as a young boy.
Branches clawed my face;
leaves brushed my shoulders,
but still I ran.

It was not long before
I arrived home,
my wife waiting by open door,
light pouring outside.
I ran to her,
took her in my arms as
I closed the door.
Heart pounding,
tears in my eyes,
I laughed as I told my wife
how I had run like
a scared child.

But my sweet wife
did not share in my laughter.
It was then she told me,
lips trembling,
how she'd seen
an ominous shadow
chasing me out of the forest
just moments before

I closed the door –
a shadow so dark
yet unmistakably alive,
a shadow with wings.

On a clear night, I weep
beneath the ghosts of dead stars.

Six Feet Under

Four-man detail
disembarks spacecraft
hesitant yet determined,
afraid yet eager,
for this is an expedition unlike
any other.

The ground feels soft,
and they amble clumsily
in bulky suits.
A crew member crouches,
taking samples for tests.

Photos taken via
remote satellite
show no visible life
on the surface.
No terrestrial creatures
nor any in the sky.

For months they have
travelled across
the far reaches of space,
leaving their home planet
in search of a new one .

On the horizon,
rock formations jut like
gigantic tombstones –

grave markers in this cold
and desolate place.

The ground shifts.
Someone screams,
quickly followed by
the frantic voices
of the frightened crew.
The surface quakes.

Powerful cameras detected
nothing on the planet surface,
but what they had not uncovered
was the teeming,
hungry life below.

I stand before you,
unnoticed after all this time.

Bad Tip

The manor sits
like a lonely monarch
atop the hill –
grand, yet distant.

Riches and fortune,
it is said, lie in wait for
people who seek them –
and those who aren't
afraid of serving
a ten-year jail sentence.

Blowtorch cuts
through inches
of steel.
Red hot metal runs
like cheap, dripping
nail polish.

Heavy vault door
swings open,
and a shadow blossoms
In the wan light.
Thief trips backward
as his reward lurches
into view.

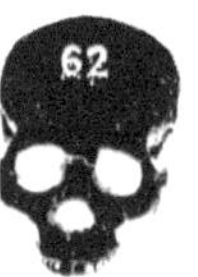

Not all locked doors
hide treasure and wealth;
some are meant to keep
terrible secrets
locked away.

When You Have Nothing Nice to Say

Around the television,
family gathers –
Dad in his leather reading chair,
Mom and Debby on the sofa,
and Alex with his
plastic toy soldiers
on the living room floor.

The evening game show
is interrupted by breaking news;
another local resident
found dead
in the woods –
the third in a week.

Dad shakes his head,
goes on default mode,
and blames the government.
The grim news frightens Mom
who decides to turn in early.

Alex couldn't care less –
his green plastic troops
all over the ground.
Debby realizes she cannot tell
the good guys
from the bad.

Later that night,
lying alone in darkness

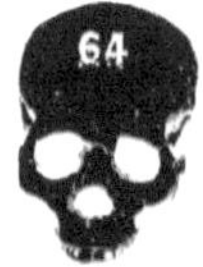

in her bedroom
Debby's thoughts wander
to the dead man
on TV.

He did not suffer much,
she hopes,
but her conscience
says otherwise.
An unbearable burden
weighs heavily on her chest.

Tears blot sheets
as she curses the day
she discovered
the seemingly harmless book
and uttered the arcane words
contained within
the tattered pages.

Tumbleweed

Blood seeps through
narrow gaps
between wooden planks,
like syrup on a stack of
pancakes.

Johnny lies not far away
convulsing on the saloon floor,
torn arm squirting
more crimson fluid,
life literally draining away
from his body.

Slowly, pistol drawn,
I back away toward the bar
at the far end of the building.
Outside, the horses are
throwing a fit.

I sweep the gun
left and right.
Johnny has stopped moving.
He's dead;
they all are.
It's just me
and that thing outside.

upon scorched earth
first drops of rain
ambulance wails
in the distance

Drowse

Eyelids heavy
but mind refuses to relent,
for whatever dangers
there are in
the waking world
pale in comparison
to those that lurk
in the shadowy realms
of dreams and nightmares.

Stifled yawn;
entire body trembles
with weariness.
My fatigued brain
recalls creatures scuttling,
slithering in the dark,
nightmarish monstrosities
hanging from the ceiling,
shifting and jostling
with hungry anticipation.

I take a deep breath
to bring much-needed
oxygen to my lethargic mind.
I must not sleep;
I cannot!
Cannot fall under
the claws and teeth that await.
I cannot.
I can...

Stuck

Yesterday,
I saw you when you were born,
fragile, delicate, and loud,
naive to the ways of the world.

A week ago,
I witnessed your first steps –
hesitant at first, clumsy,
but more confident
with each stride as if
you already knew
where you were going.

Two days ago,
I watched them bury you.
the ceremony was solemn,
and all your friends were there.
You would have approved.
Even I shed a tear.

Like a broken record,
we find ourselves
stuck in the same cycle,
reliving a loop
over and over,
until the grooves are
so scratched and worn,
we give in to madness.

As you point the gun

to my head,
the end of the barrel as dark
as the nothingness
that follows death,
I smile,
for we have been here before.

Team Spirit

Students used to cheer
and look up to the players.
There was a time
when the gym would
fill to capacity and
the roar of the crowd
could be heard
from miles away.

Those were the days.
Now, we'd be lucky
to fill half the seats.
Students would rather
stay home and watch Netflix
or update their Facebook
and Instagram accounts.
We have lost our
team spirit.

It broke my heart
when we lost the Regionals
by only three points.
For all our hard work,
all the school had
to show for it was a poorly
written column by a student
who spelled half
the players' names wrong.

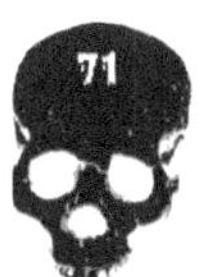

To me, that article
hurt as much as losing
the game.

I wander the hallways
in my team jacket
wondering when it
had all gone wrong.
When did we lose sight
of the important things?
The pistol tucked
in the waist of my pants
weighs heavy
as I walk into class.
My pulse races as if
I am about to take
a winning shot.
This will not end well,
of that, I'm aware;
but I'm willing to
take one for the team.

Tread Softly for the Dead Sleep

In earthen graves,
beyond the reaches
of light,
worms have their fill
in darkness.

A hundred corpses,
nameless and long-forgotten,
decompose beyond
recognition,
rendering the soil fertile
while others,
dry and pulverized,
return to the raw material
from which it is said
Man was fashioned.

High above on the surface,
upon a bright blanket
spread next to a patch
of yellow dandelions,
a man and woman embrace,
unaware of that which
eternally slumbers.

The Man Who Played With Dolls

Glass eyes
and porcelain faces –
inanimate audience
watches, unblinking.

For over half his life
the doll maker has perfected
his craft.
Each of his creations –
as unique as any living child –
has brought a smile
to the man's face.

But children grow up,
and toys do not last
forever.
Innocence is lost,
and his creations are
destined to rot away
in basements and attics.

Four decades –
half a lifetime;
the man who plays with dolls,
lonely amongst rows and shelves
of silent family members,
decides to play no longer.

Like the dolls
that surround him,
he, too, was not meant
to last.

tyrant announces
vaccine finally approved
no one left to save

Pathogen

Cold metal surfaces
reflect overhead light.
Machines – centrifuges, incubators,
refrigerators, computers –
issue a solemn
chorus of hums.

Warriors humbly bow
their heads and peer
through microscope lenses
for a deeper understanding
of the monsters
plaguing humanity –
demons that exist
but dwell, hidden from
the naked eye.

Cloaked with hazmat suits
and sterile gloves,
anointed with Povidone
and alcohol,
new age soldiers
forge on,
battling the unseen foe –
monsters in petri dishes
and ghouls swirling
inside test tubes.

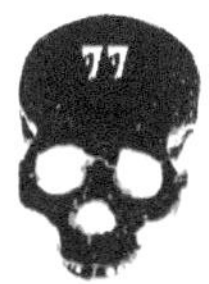

wilted bouquet
adorns empty grave
Grandpa on the loose

About the Poet

Aurelio Rico Lopez III hails from Iloilo City, Philippines. He is the author of *Not the Forgiving Kind*, *Kaiju Double Barrel*, *Night Mare*, *No Grave Too Deep*, *Hangover of the Apocalypse*, and *Wretched*. His poetry collections include *Two Drinks Away From Chaos*, *When the Lights Go Out*, and *The Odd Ones*. Aurelio is a self-diagnosed scribble junkie whose addictions include doughnuts, coffee, books, and horror movies.

Hybrid Sequence Media Bibliography

001- Bring Something Dead

002- Meat Grinder

003- From the Belly of the Goat

004- Mr. Miyagi's Soggy Cereal

005- Separation: Healing

006- Rogue

007- Shrapnel

008- The Word For Poetry Is Poetry

009- Catacomb Kittens

0010- Bottomlands

0011- Emotional Time-Lapse

0012- Chicken Lust

9 798721 991509